Hall of Mirrors

Hall of Mirrors
Fredric Brown

ÆGYPAN PRESS

Special thanks to Greg Weeks, Stephen Blundell, and the
Online Distributed Proofreading Team (which can be found
at http://www.pgdp.net).

This story first appeared in the December 1953 issue of
Galaxy Science Fiction.

Hall of Mirrors
A publication of
ÆGYPAN PRESS

www.aegypan.com

It is a tough decision to make — whether to give up your life so you can live it over again!

*F*or an instant you think it is temporary blindness, this sudden dark that comes in the middle of a bright afternoon.

It *must* be blindness, you think; could the sun that was tanning you have gone out instantaneously, leaving you in utter blackness?

Then the nerves of your body tell you that you are *standing*, whereas only a second ago you were sitting comfortably, almost reclining, in a canvas chair. In the patio of a friend's house in Beverly Hills. Talking to Barbara, your fiancée. Looking at Barbara — Barbara in a swim suit — her skin golden tan in the brilliant sunshine, beautiful.

You wore swimming trunks. Now you do not feel them on you; the slight pressure of the elastic waistband is no longer there against your waist. You touch your hands to your hips. You are naked. And standing.

Whatever has happened to you is more than a change to sudden darkness or to sudden blindness.

You raise your hands gropingly before you. They touch a plain smooth surface, a wall. You spread them apart and each hand reaches a corner. You pivot slowly. A second wall, then a third, then a door. You are in a closet about four feet square.

Your hand finds the knob of the door. It turns and you push the door open.

There is light now. The door has opened to a lighted room . . . a room that you have never seen before.

*I*t is not large, but it is pleasantly furnished — although the furniture is of a style that is strange to you. Modesty makes you open the door cautiously the rest of the way. But the room is empty of people.

You step into the room, turning to look behind you into the closet, which is now illuminated by light from the room. The closet is and is not a closet; it is the size and shape of one, but it contains nothing, not a single hook, no rod for hanging clothes, no shelf. It is an empty, blank-walled, four-by-four-foot space.

You close the door to it and stand looking around the room. It is about twelve by sixteen feet. There is one door, but it is closed. There are no windows. Five pieces of furniture. Four of them you recognize — more or less. One looks like a very functional desk. One is obviously a chair . . . a comfortable-looking one. There is a table, although its top is on several levels instead of only one. Another is a bed, or couch. Something shimmering is lying across it and you walk over and pick the shimmering something up and examine it. It is a garment.

You are naked, so you put it on. Slippers are part way under the bed (or couch) and you slide your feet into them. They fit, and they feel warm and comfortable as nothing you have ever worn on your feet has felt. Like lamb's wool, but softer.

You are dressed now. You look at the door — the only door of the room except that of the closet (closet?) from which you entered it. You walk to the door and before you try the knob, you see the small typewritten sign pasted just above it that reads:

This door has a time lock set to open in one hour. For reasons you will soon understand, it is better that you do not leave this room before then. There is a letter for you on the desk. Please read it.

It is not signed. You look at the desk and see that there is an envelope lying on it.

You do not yet go to take that envelope from the desk and read the letter that must be in it.

Why not? Because you are frightened.

You see other things about the room. The lighting has no source that you can discover. It comes from nowhere. It is not indirect lighting; the ceiling and the walls are not reflecting it at all.

[Illustration: Illustrated by VIDMER]

They didn't have lighting like that, back where you came from. What did you mean by *back where you came from?*

You close your eyes. You tell yourself: *I am Norman Hastings. I am an associate professor of mathematics at the University of Southern California. I am twenty-five years old, and this is the year nineteen hundred and fifty-four.*

You open your eyes and look again.

*T*hey didn't use that style of furniture in Los Angeles — or anywhere else that you know of — in 1954. That thing over in the corner — you can't even guess what it is. So might your grandfather, at your age, have looked at a television set.

You look down at yourself, at the shimmering garment that you found waiting for you. With thumb and forefinger you feel its texture.

It's like nothing you've ever touched before.

I am Norman Hastings. This is nineteen hundred and fifty-four.

Suddenly you must know, and at once.

You go to the desk and pick up the envelope that lies upon it. Your name is typed on the outside: *Norman Hastings.*

Your hands shake a little as you open it. Do you blame them?

There are several pages, typewritten. Dear Norman, it starts. You turn quickly to the end to look for the signature. It is unsigned.

You turn back and start reading.

"Do not be afraid. There is nothing to fear, but much to explain. Much that you must understand before the time lock opens that door. Much that you must accept and — obey.

"You have already guessed that you are in the future — in what, to you, seems to be the future. The clothes and the room must have told you that. I planned it that way so the shock would not be too sudden, so you would realize it over the course of several minutes rather than read it here — and quite probably disbelieve what you read.

"The 'closet' from which you have just stepped is, as you have by now realized, a time machine. From it you stepped into the world of 2004. The date is April 7th, just fifty years from the time you last remember.

"You cannot return.

"I did this to you and you may hate me for it; I do not know. That is up to you to decide, but it does not matter. What does matter, and not to you alone, is another decision which you must make. I am incapable of making it.

"Who is writing this to you? I would rather not tell you just yet. By the time you have finished reading this, even though it is not signed (for I knew you would look first for a signature), I will not need to tell you who I am. You will know.

"I am seventy-five years of age. I have, in this year 2004, been studying 'time' for thirty of those years. I have completed the first time machine ever built — and thus far, its construction, even the fact that it has been constructed, is my own secret.

"You have just participated in the first major experiment. It will be your responsibility to decide whether there shall ever be anymore experiments with it, whether it should be given to the world, or whether it should be destroyed and never used again."

*E*nd of the first page. You look up for a moment, hesitating to turn the next page. Already you suspect what is coming.

You turn the page.

"I constructed the first time machine a week ago. My calculations had told me that it would work, but not how it would work. I had expected it to send an object back in time — it works backward in time only, not forward — physically unchanged and intact.

"My first experiment showed me my error. I placed a cube of metal in the machine — it was a miniature of the one you just walked out of — and set the machine to go backward ten years. I flicked the switch and opened the door, expecting to find the cube vanished. Instead I found it had crumbled to powder.

"I put in another cube and sent it two years back. The second cube came back unchanged, except that it was newer, shinier.

"That gave me the answer. I had been expecting the cubes to go back in time, and they had done so, but not in the sense I had expected them to. Those metal cubes had been fabricated about three years previously. I had sent the first one back years before it had existed in its fabricated form. Ten years ago it had been ore. The machine returned it to that state.

"Do you see how our previous theories of time travel have been wrong? We expected to be able to step into a time machine in, say, 2004, set it for fifty years back, and then step out in the year 1954 . . . but it does not work that way. The machine does not move in time. Only whatever is within the machine is affected, and then just with relation to itself and not to the rest of the Universe.

"I confirmed this with guinea pigs by sending one six weeks old five weeks back and it came out a baby.

"I need not outline all my experiments here. You will find a record of them in the desk and you can study it later.

"Do you understand now what has happened to you, Norman?"

*Y*ou begin to understand. And you begin to sweat.

The *I* who wrote that letter you are now reading is *you*, yourself at the age of seventy-five, in this year of 2004. You are that seventy-five-year-old man, with your body returned to what it had been fifty years ago, with all the memories of fifty years of living wiped out.

You invented the time machine.

And before you used it on yourself, you made these arrangements to help you orient yourself. You wrote yourself the letter which you are now reading.

But if those fifty years are — to you — gone, what of all your friends, those you loved? What of your parents? What of the girl you are going — were going — to marry?

You read on:

"Yes, you will want to know what has happened. Mom died in 1963, Dad in 1968. You married Barbara in 1956. I am sorry to tell you that she died only three years later, in a plane crash. You have one son. He is still living; his name is Walter; he is now forty-six years old and is an accountant in Kansas City."

Tears come into your eyes and for a moment you can no longer read. Barbara dead — dead for forty-five years. And only minutes ago, in subjective time, you were sitting next to her, sitting in the bright sun in a Beverly Hills patio . . .

You force yourself to read again.

"But back to the discovery. You begin to see some of its implications. You will need time to think to see all of them.

"It does not permit time travel as we have thought of time travel, but it gives us immortality of a sort. Immortality of the kind I have temporarily given us.

"*Is it good?* Is it worth while to lose the memory of fifty years of one's life in order to return one's body to relative youth? The only way I can find out is to try, as soon as I have finished writing this and made my other preparations.

"You will know the answer.

"But before you decide, remember that there is another problem, more important than the psychological one. I mean overpopulation.

"If our discovery is given to the world, if all who are old or dying can make themselves young again, the population will almost double every generation. Nor would the world — not even our own relatively enlightened country — be willing to accept compulsory birth control as a solution.

"Give this to the world, as the world is today in 2004, and within a generation there will be famine, suffering, war. Perhaps a complete collapse of civilization.

"Yes, we have reached other planets, but they are not suitable for colonizing. The stars may be our answer, but we are a long way from reaching them. When we do, someday, the billions of habitable planets that must be out there will be our answer . . . our living room. But until then, what is the answer?

"Destroy the machine? But think of the countless lives it can save, the suffering it can prevent. Think of what it would mean to a man dying of cancer. Think . . ."

*T*hink. You finish the letter and put it down.

You think of Barbara dead for forty-five years. And of the fact that you were married to her for three years and that those years are lost to you.

Fifty years lost. You damn the old man of seventy-five whom you became and who has done this to you . . . who has given you this decision to make.

Bitterly, you know what the decision must be. You think that *he* knew, too, and realize that he could safely leave it in your hands. Damn him, he *should* have known.

Too valuable to destroy, too dangerous to give.

The other answer is painfully obvious.

You must be custodian of this discovery and keep it secret until it is safe to give, until mankind has expanded to the stars and has new worlds to populate, or until, even without that, he has reached a state of civilization where he can avoid overpopulation by rationing births to the number of accidental — or voluntary — deaths.

If neither of those things has happened in another fifty years (and are they likely so soon?), then you, at seventy-five, will be writing another letter like this one. You will be undergoing another experience similar to the one you're going through now. And making the same decision, of course.

Why not? You'll be the same person again.

Time and again, to preserve this secret until Man is ready for it.

How often will you again sit at a desk like this one, thinking the thoughts you are thinking now, feeling the grief you now feel?

There is a click at the door and you know that the time lock has opened, that you are now free to leave this room, free to start a new life for yourself in place of the one you have already lived and lost.

But you are in no hurry now to walk directly through that door.

You sit there, staring straight ahead of you blindly, seeing in your mind's eye the vista of a set of facing mirrors, like those in an old-fashioned barber shop, reflecting the same thing over and over again, diminishing into far distance.

— FREDRIC BROWN